The Most Wonderful Egg in the World

Originally published under the title: *Das Schönste Ei der Welt* by Helme Heine
by Gertraud Middelhauve Verlag, Köln
Copyright © 1983 by Gertraud Middelhauve Verlag, Köln
English translation copyright © 1983 by J. M. Dent & Sons, Ltd London

Aladdin Books
Macmillan Publishing Company
866 Third Avenue, New York, NY 10022
Collier Macmillan Canada, Inc.

Printed in the United States of America
A hardcover edition of *The Most Wonderful Egg in the World* is available from
Margaret K. McElderry Books, Macmillan Publishing Company.
First Aladdin Books edition 1987
10 9 8 7 6 5 4 3 2 1

Library of Congress Cataloging-in-Publication Data

Heine, Helme.
The most wonderful egg in the world.

Translation of: Das schönste Ei der Welt.
Summary: To settle a quarrel between three hens, the king must choose which one lays
the most beautiful egg.
[1. Chickens—Fiction. 2. Beauty, Personal—Fiction]
I. Title.
PZ7.H3678Mo   1987   [E]   86-22251
ISBN 0-689-71117-4

The Most Wonderful Egg in the World

written and illustrated by Helme Heine

Aladdin Books
Macmillan Publishing Company
New York

Once upon a time, a long time ago, three hens were quarreling about which of them was the most beautiful.

Dotty had the most beautiful feathers.

Stalky had the most beautiful legs.

And Plumy had the most beautiful crest.

Since they could not settle their quarrel among themselves, they decided to ask the king for his advice.

"What you can do is more important than what you look like," said the king. "Whichever one of you lays the most wonderful egg I will make a princess."

He went out into the palace park followed by all the
hens in his kingdom.

Dotty preened her beautiful feathers before settling herself in the wet grass. It was not long before she cackled, stood up, and stepped aside.

Everybody was speechless. There lay an egg, snow-white, spotless, and perfectly shaped—the eggshell shimmering like polished marble. "This is the most perfect egg I have ever seen," cried the king, and all the hens nodded.

Then it was Stalky's turn. Everybody felt a little
sorry for her. They knew she could not lay a more
perfect egg. It was impossible.

After ten minutes Stalky cackled, got up and
stretched her legs proudly in the morning sun.

The king clapped his hands for joy. There lay an egg of such size and weight that even an ostrich would have been jealous.

"This is the biggest egg I have ever seen," cried the
king, and all the hens nodded.

While they were still nodding, Plumy settled herself carefully on the ground. Everybody felt extremely sorry for her. They knew she could not lay a more perfect or bigger egg. It was unthinkable. Modestly, with castdown eyes, she sat there.

Then, with only a small cackle, she got up to reveal an egg that would be talked about for the next hundred years.

Before them lay a square egg. Each side was straight, as if drawn with a ruler, and each surface shone in a different color.

"This is indeed the most fantastic egg I have ever seen," cried the king, and all the hens nodded.

It was impossible to say which egg was the most wonderful. So the king decided that all three hens — Dotty, Stalky and Plumy — should be made princesses.

And from that day to this they have been the best
of friends, and have happily gone on laying
extraordinary eggs.